THE CASE OF THE
Growing
Bird Feeder

ERIC HOGAN & TARA HUNGERFORD

FIREFLY BOOKS

**FOR WILFRED, PARIS
& THEIR COUSINS.**

A FIREFLY BOOK

Published Under License by Firefly Books Ltd. 2019
Copyright © 2019 Gumboot Kids Media Inc.
Book adaptation and realization © 2019 Firefly Books Ltd.
Photographs © Gumboot Kids Media Inc. unless otherwise
specified on page 32.

This book is based on the popular children's shows *Scout &
the Gumboot Kids*, *Daisy & the Gumboot Kids* and *Jessie &
the Gumboot Kids*.

'GUMBOOT KIDS' is a trademark of Gumboot Kids Media Inc., and
an application for registration is pending in Canada. Trademarks
of Gumboot Kids Media Inc. may not be used without express
permission.

First printing

Library of Congress Control Number: 2019930772

Library and Archives Canada Cataloguing in Publication:
Title: The case of the growing bird feeder / Eric Hogan & Tara
Hungerford.
Other titles: Scout & the Gumboot Kids (Television program)
Names: Hogan, Eric, 1979- author. | Hungerford, Tara, 1975-
author. | Imagine Create Media, issuing body.
Description: Series statement: A Gumboot Kids nature mystery |
Based on the TV series: Scout & the Gumboot Kids.
Identifiers: Canadiana 20190055782 | ISBN 9780228101895
(hardcover) | ISBN 9780228101901 (softcover)
Subjects: LCSH: Sunflowers—Life cycles—Juvenile literature.
Classification: LCC QK495.C74 H64 2019 | DDC j583/.983—dc23

Published in the United States by
Firefly Books (U.S.) Inc.
P.O. Box 1338, Ellicott Station
Buffalo, New York 14205

Published in Canada by
Firefly Books Ltd.
50 Staples Avenue, Unit 1
Richmond Hill, Ontario L4B 0A7

Printed in Canada

Canada We acknowledge the financial support of the
Government of Canada.

It's a beautiful summer day. Daisy and Scout arrive at the park for a picnic.

"It's so bright and sunny," says Daisy. "Let's find a nice spot in the shade."

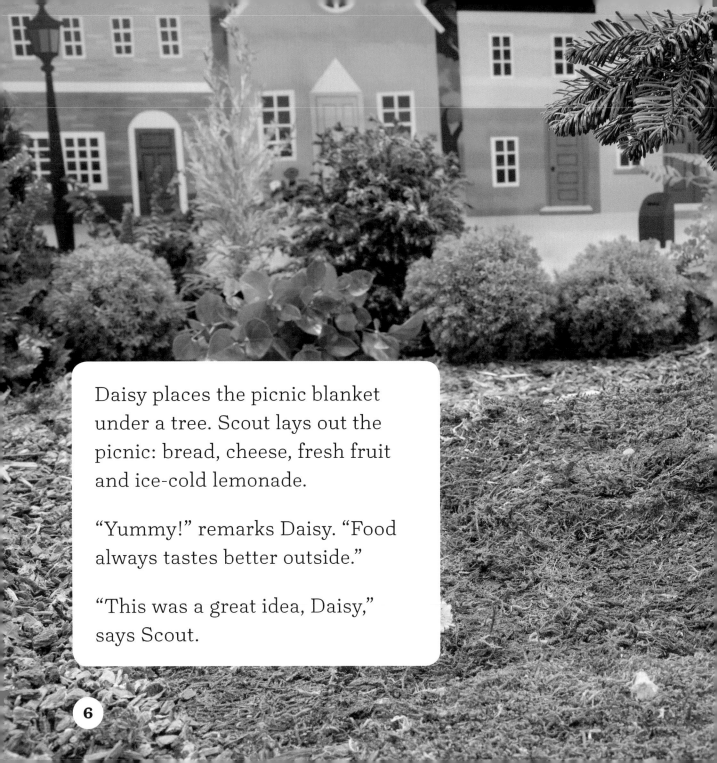

Daisy places the picnic blanket under a tree. Scout lays out the picnic: bread, cheese, fresh fruit and ice-cold lemonade.

"Yummy!" remarks Daisy. "Food always tastes better outside."

"This was a great idea, Daisy," says Scout.

The birds chirp in the tree overhead.
"I love hearing the birds sing," says Scout.

"Me too," agrees Daisy. "Which reminds me,
I forgot to water my bird feeders today."

"Water your bird feeders? What do you
mean?" asks Scout.

Daisy smiles. "I need to water my bird feeders
so that they grow tall and stay healthy."

"What kind of bird feeders grow?" asks Scout.

"I'm not telling," replies Daisy. "But I will help
you solve the nature mystery."

"Ooh," says Scout. "The Case of the Growing
Bird Feeder."

"Here, I sketched a few clues for you," says Daisy, showing Scout her field notes.

"A garden. Hmm, I know a lovely garden that's not too far from here," says Scout. "Follow me!"

Garden

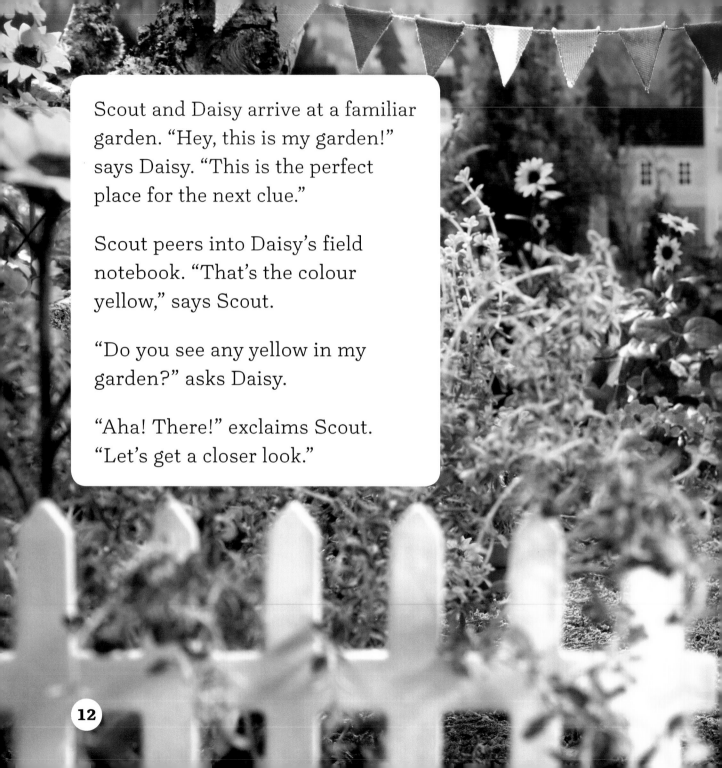

Scout and Daisy arrive at a familiar garden. "Hey, this is my garden!" says Daisy. "This is the perfect place for the next clue."

Scout peers into Daisy's field notebook. "That's the colour yellow," says Scout.

"Do you see any yellow in my garden?" asks Daisy.

"Aha! There!" exclaims Scout. "Let's get a closer look."

Yellow

"What interesting flowers," says Scout.

"Here's another clue" says Daisy, pointing to her field notes. "Seeds."

Scout leans in with his magnifying glass.

"Check it out!" says Scout. "The seeds are right inside the flower head. Incredible! This is definitely a sunflower."

Seeds

"Now, can you put the clues together to solve The Case of the Growing Bird Feeder?" asks Daisy.

"Well, let's see," begins Scout. "In the garden we found yellow flowers — sunflowers — with seeds... Hey Daisy, didn't you say you needed to water your bird feeders?"

"Yes I did!" says Daisy.

Scout and Daisy fill a big watering can and pour water around each of the sunflowers.

A bird flies down and lands on a sunflower. Scout and Daisy look up at it in astonishment.

"Look, Scout!" says Daisy.

"Wow! That bird is eating the sunflower seeds!" exclaims Scout. "I've got it! The sunflower is the growing bird feeder!"

"Well done, Scout!" says Daisy. "Let's go inside and check out my library book about sunflowers."

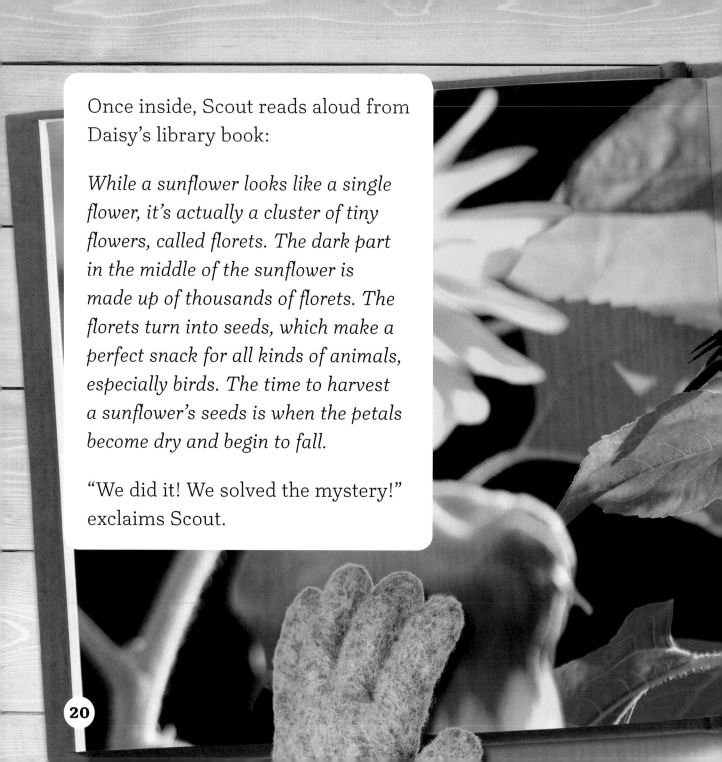

Once inside, Scout reads aloud from Daisy's library book:

While a sunflower looks like a single flower, it's actually a cluster of tiny flowers, called florets. The dark part in the middle of the sunflower is made up of thousands of florets. The florets turn into seeds, which make a perfect snack for all kinds of animals, especially birds. The time to harvest a sunflower's seeds is when the petals become dry and begin to fall.

"We did it! We solved the mystery!" exclaims Scout.

Sunflower seeds

Back in Daisy's Garden, Scout and Daisy pause and have a mindful moment.

"Throughout the day, a sunflower's head turns to follow the sun," Daisy tells Scout. "Let's pretend to be sunflowers! Stand tall, close your eyes and face toward the sun. Feel the sun's warmth on your skin, take a deep breath and smile. Ahh!"

"I feel grateful for the sunshine," says Scout. "It helps the garden grow — and it makes me feel happy."

"I really worked up an appetite solving this nature mystery. I sure could use a snack before I walk home," says Scout.

"How about some sunflower seeds?" asks Daisy.

"I'd love some!" replies Scout.

"Here you go," says Daisy, as she gives Scout a handful of seeds.

"Thanks, Daisy! See you tomorrow for another nature mystery!"

Later, after watering all her sunflowers, Daisy picks a few to take inside.

"These will look great on my table," says Daisy. "They're a nice way to bring a little bit of sunshine inside. Goodbye for now, Gumboot Kids!"

Field Notes

Ray Florets: Each yellow petal around a sunflower head is a separate flower. These large florets are meant to attract pollinators.

Disk Florets and Seeds: The dark center is made up of thousands of brown flowers, which produce seeds once the florets have been pollinated.

Leaves: The leaves (and head) of the sunflower move to face the sun throughout the day. This is called heliotropism.

Stalk: Sunflowers can grow up to 9.8 feet (3 meters) tall.

Roots: The roots absorb water and minerals for the flowers.

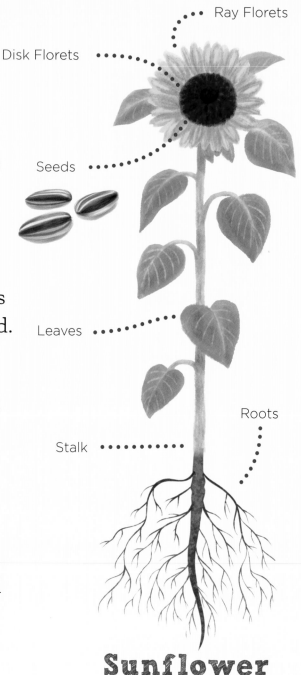

Ray Florets

Disk Florets

Seeds

Leaves

Roots

Stalk

Sunflower

Almost every part of a sunflower is edible. It is a source of food for animals and people alike.

There are almost 70 different varieties of sunflower.

Sunflowers and daisies are both in the Asteraceae family.

A sunflower may look like one big flower, but it's actually hundreds, if not thousands of tiny flowers growing together.

People have been growing sunflowers for thousands of years because they have so many uses.

Sunflowers don't just look like the sun, they need a lot of it. They are heliotropic plants, which means they move so that they are always facing toward the sun.

Nature Craft

Inspired by sunflowers, Daisy and Scout make birdseed cookies. Would you like to make some treats for the birds to eat?

STEP 1

Collect some cookie cutters from your kitchen. Choose fun shapes like stars and hearts.

STEP 2

Ask an adult to help you mix 2 cups of birdseed, two teaspoons of unflavoured gelatin and a cup of warm water in a large mixing bowl. Place your cookie cutters on a flat surface and fill them with the birdseed mixture. Use your hand to press it down to form your cookie. Use a pencil to make a hole in each cookie so you can hang them up once they're dry.

STEP 3

Let your cookies dry completely and then push them out of the cookie cutter. Tie some string through the hole of each cookie. Now hang your creation on a branch for your bird friends to enjoy!

TELEVISION SERIES CREDITS
Created by Eric Hogan and Tara Hungerford
Produced by Tracey Mack
Developed for television with Cathy Moss
Music by Jessie Farrell

Television Consultants
Mindfulness: Molly Stewart Lawlor, Ph.D
Zoology: Michelle Tseng, Ph.D
Botany: Loren Rieseberg, Ph.D

BOOK CREDITS
Based on scripts for television by Tara Hungerford, Cathy Moss and Eric Hogan
Production Design: Eric Hogan and Tara Hungerford
Head of Production: Tracey Mack
Character Animation: Deanna Partridge-David
Graphic Design: Rio Trenaman, Gurjant Singh Sekhon and Lucas Green
Photography: Sean Cox
Illustration: Kate Jeong

Special thanks to the Gumboot Kids cast and crew, CBC Kids, Shaw Rocket Fund, Independent Media Fund, The Bell Fund, Canada Media Fund, Creative BC, Playology, B. Russell, and our friends and family.

ADDITIONAL PHOTO CREDITS
30 Anick Violette (bird cookies)

Shutterstock.com
14, 16-17, 18, 22 Nataliia Melnychuk, Helmut Krb, SaKaLovo, Bachkova Natalia (sunflower heads used in composite art); 20-21 Bergamont (seeds), Nil Kulp (bird); 29 5r82 (sunflower with sunset), Kurlin Café (daisy), Tharnapoom Voranavin (florets); 30 Amornchaijj (seeds), Kaiskynet Studio (cookie cutters)

More GUMBOOT KIDS Nature Mysteries

Visit Scout and Daisy
gumbootkids.com

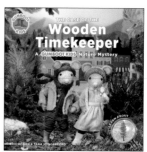